ANIMAL MANDALA
COLORING PLANET

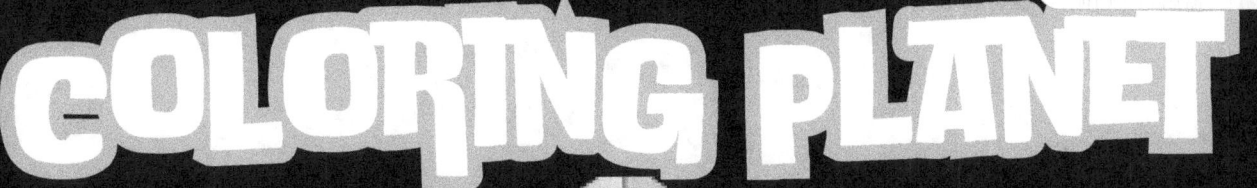

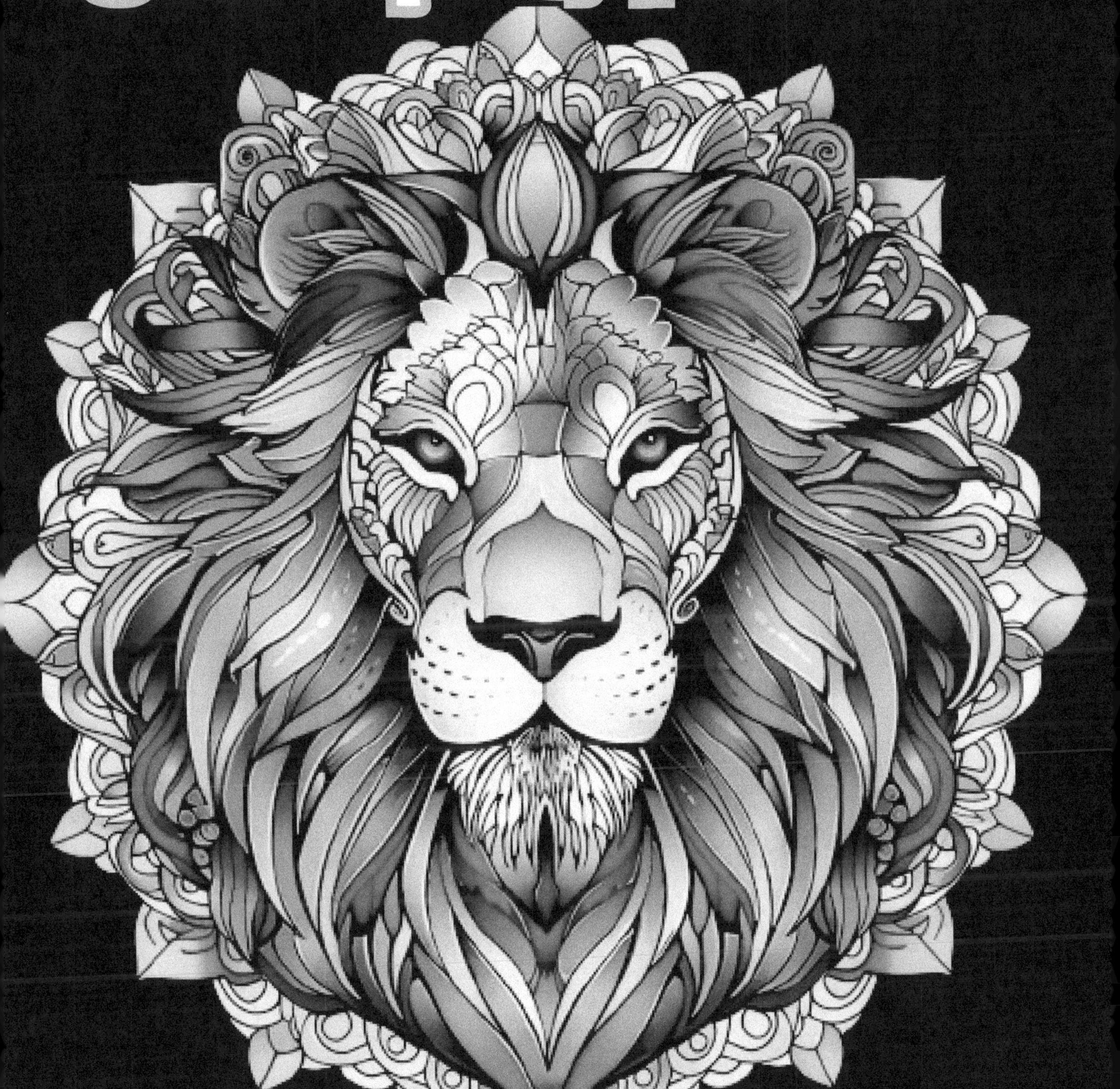

TAKEISHA HARDAWAY

ANIMAL MANDALA
COLORING PLANET

978-1-960815-90-3
PUBLISH BY:

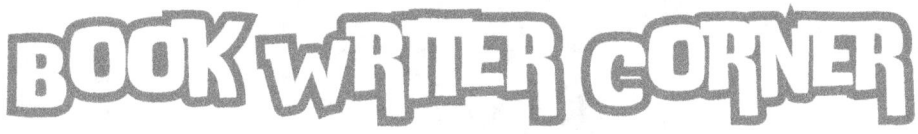

BOOK WRITTER CORNER

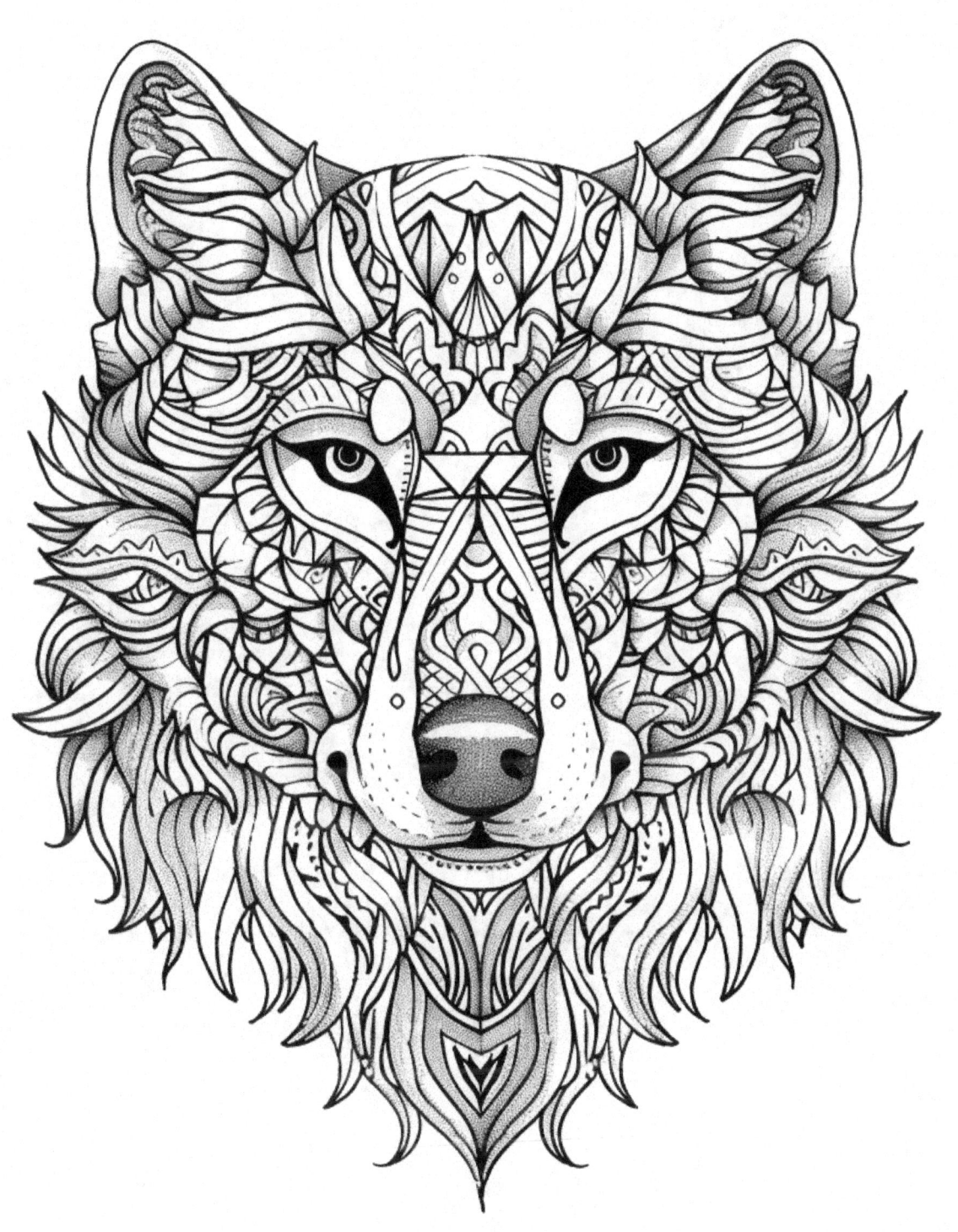

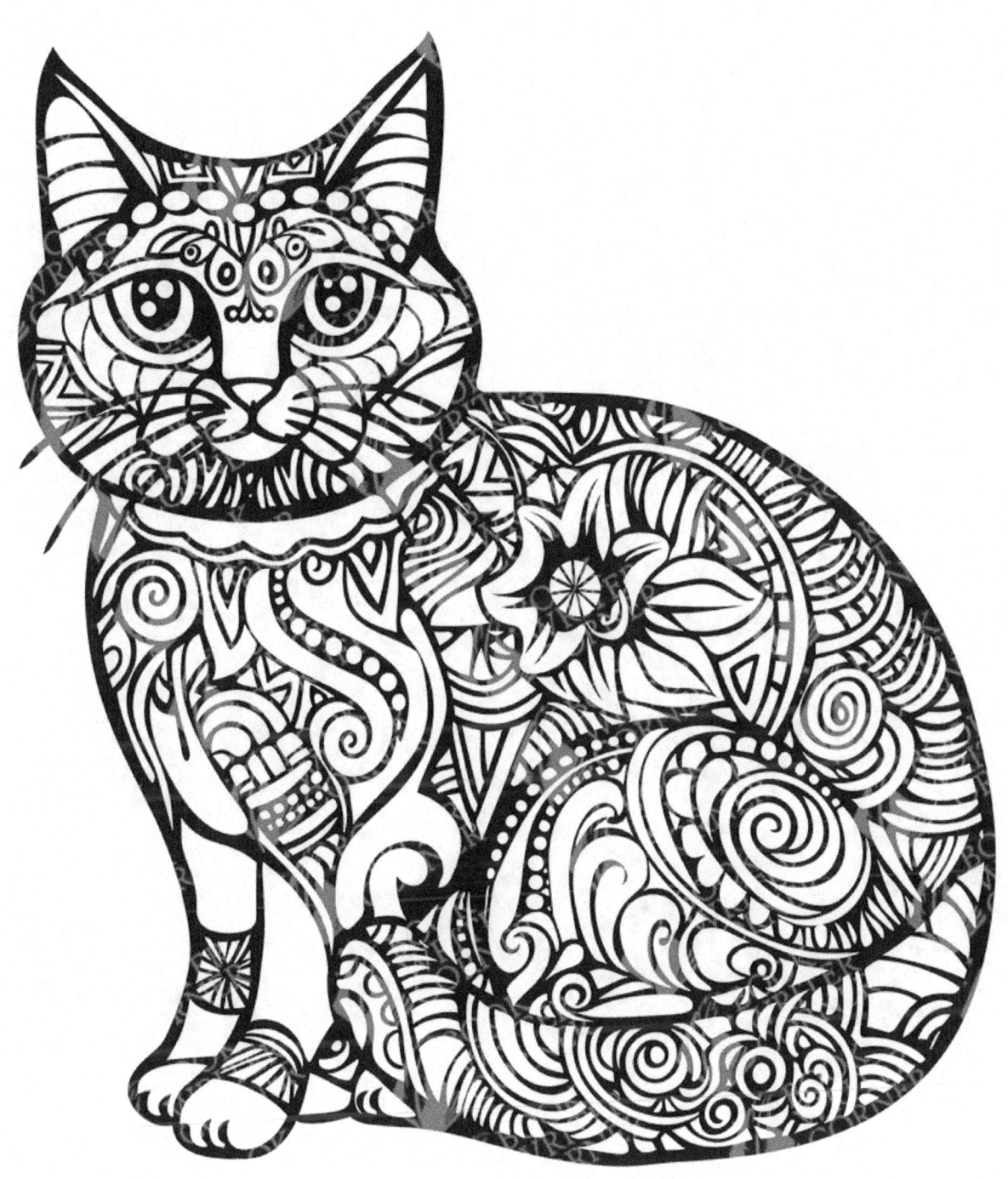

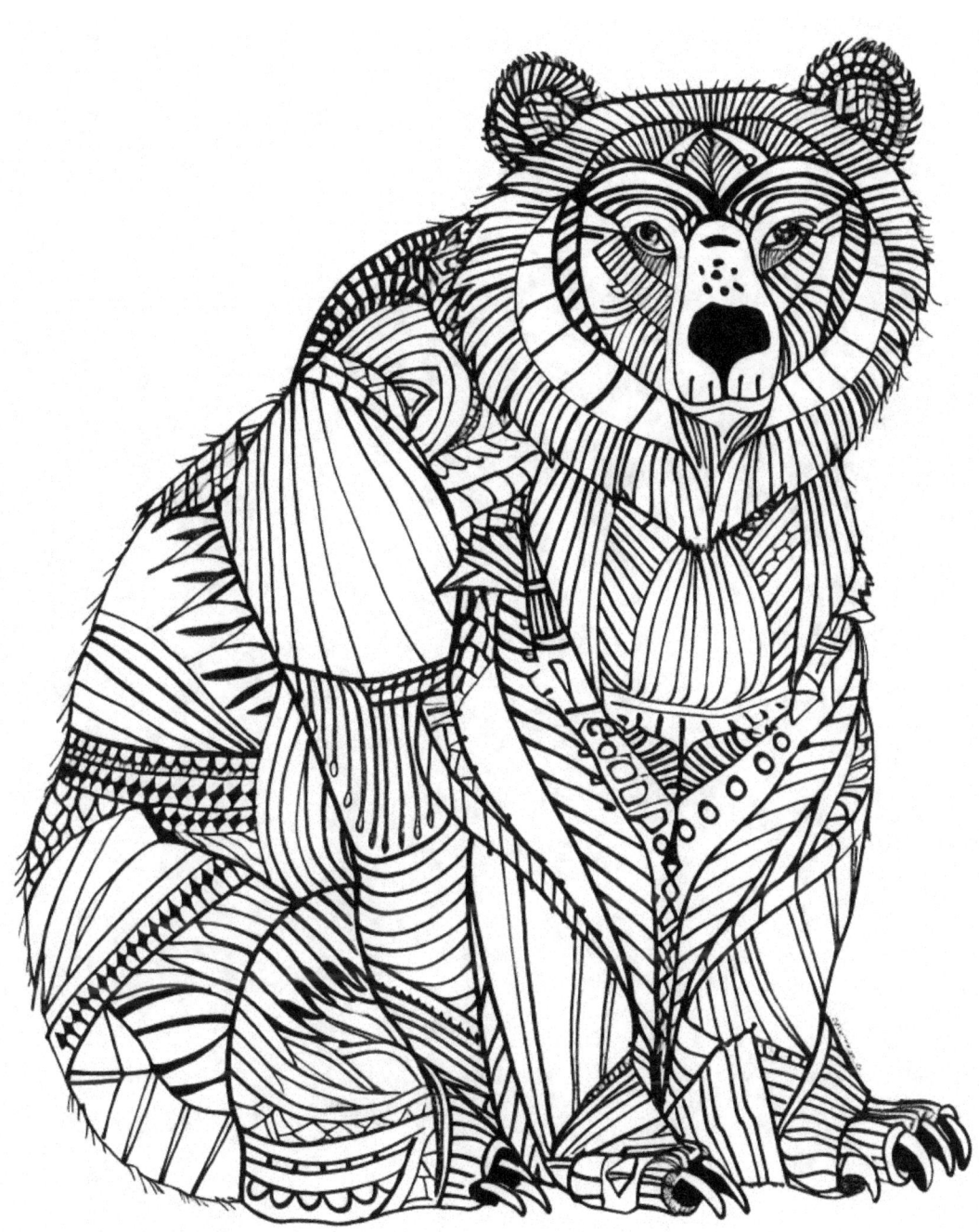

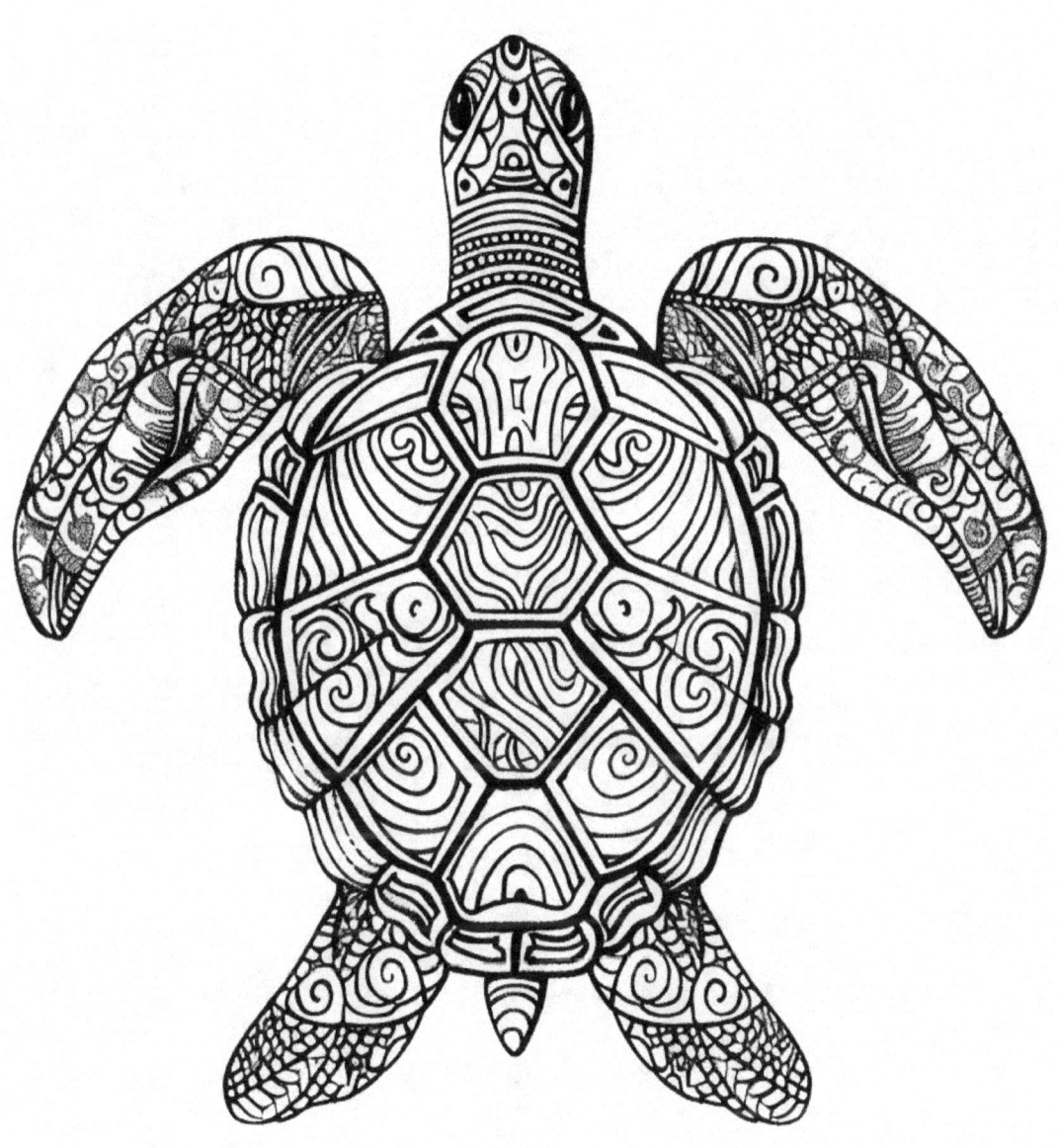

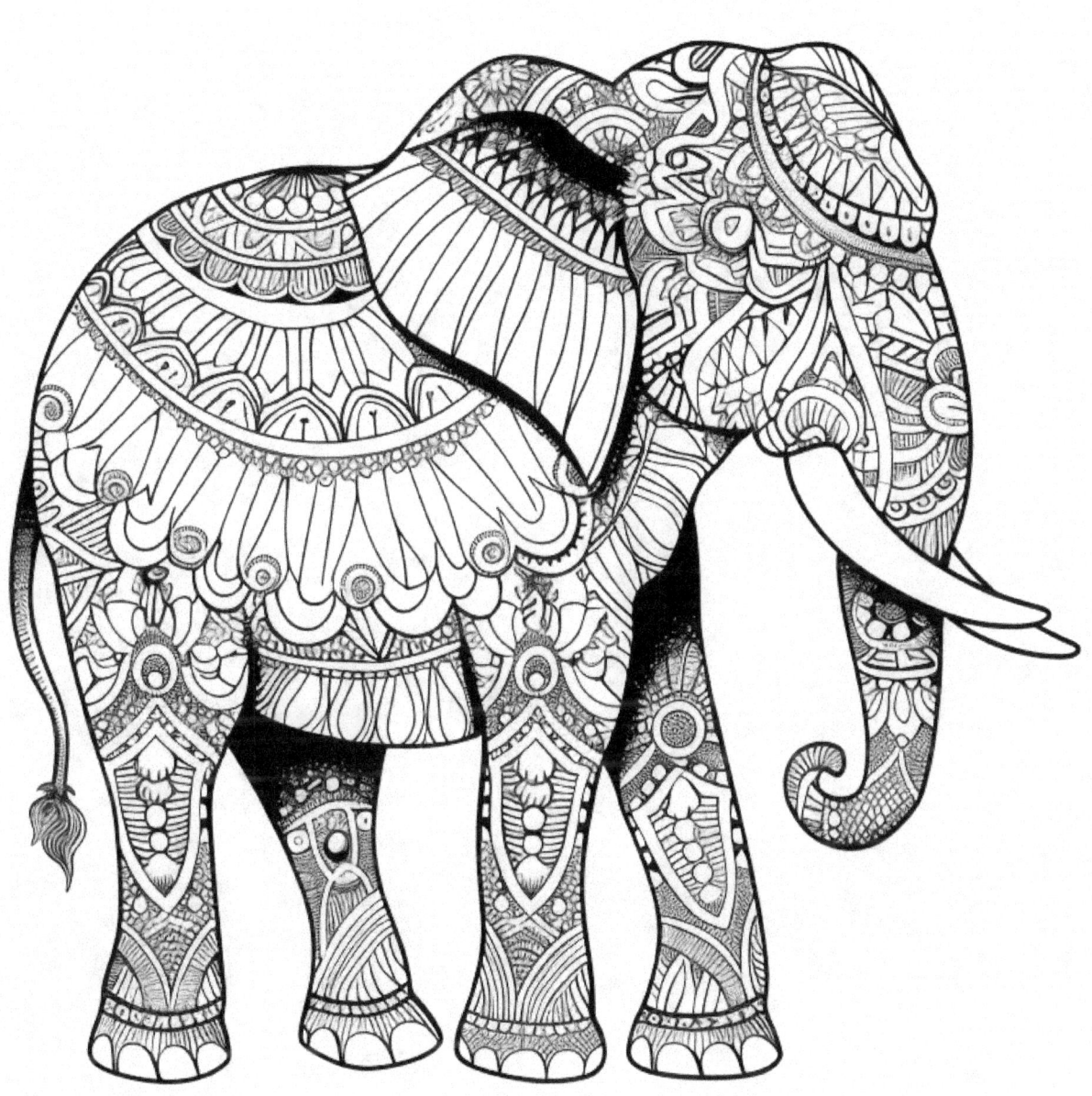

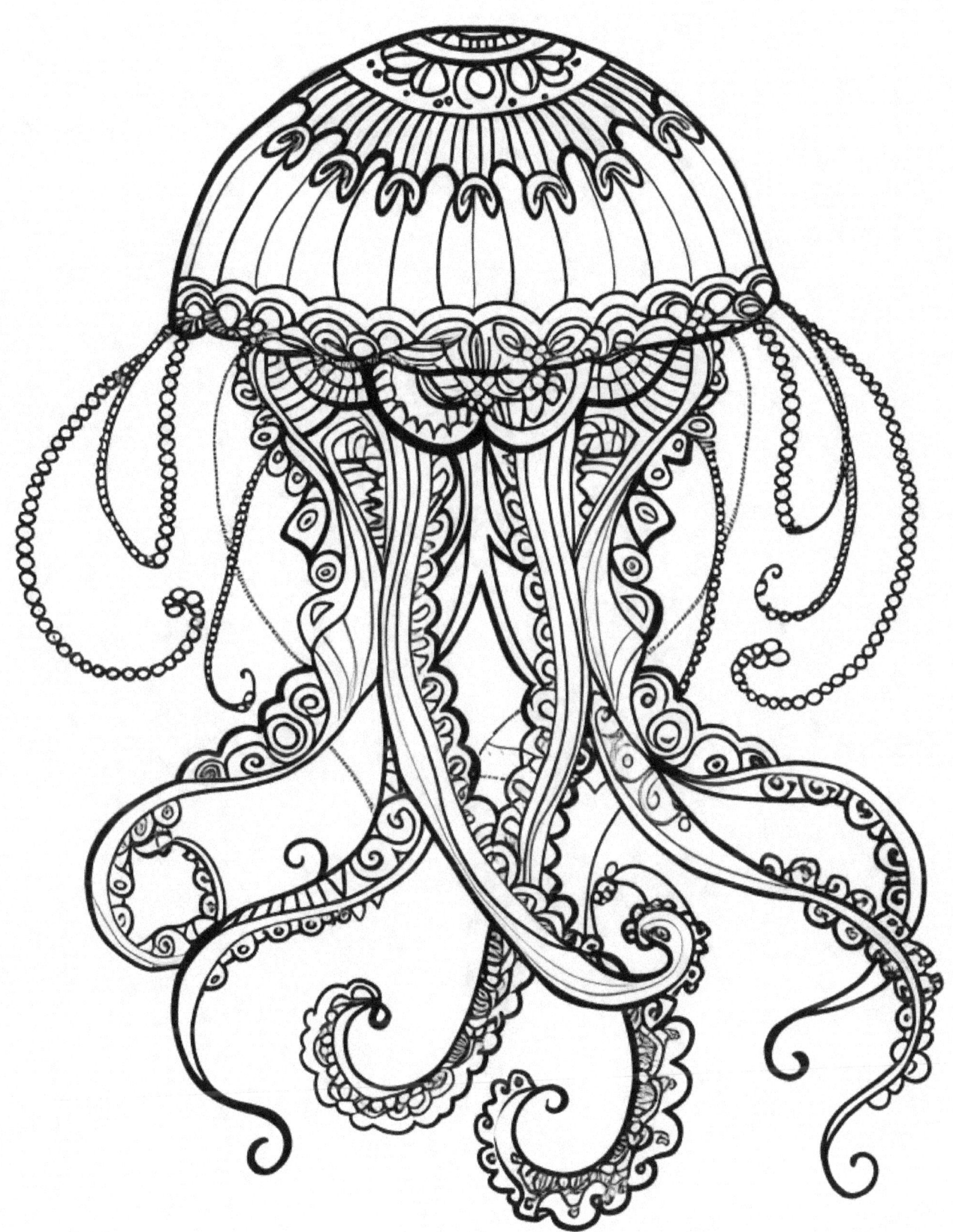

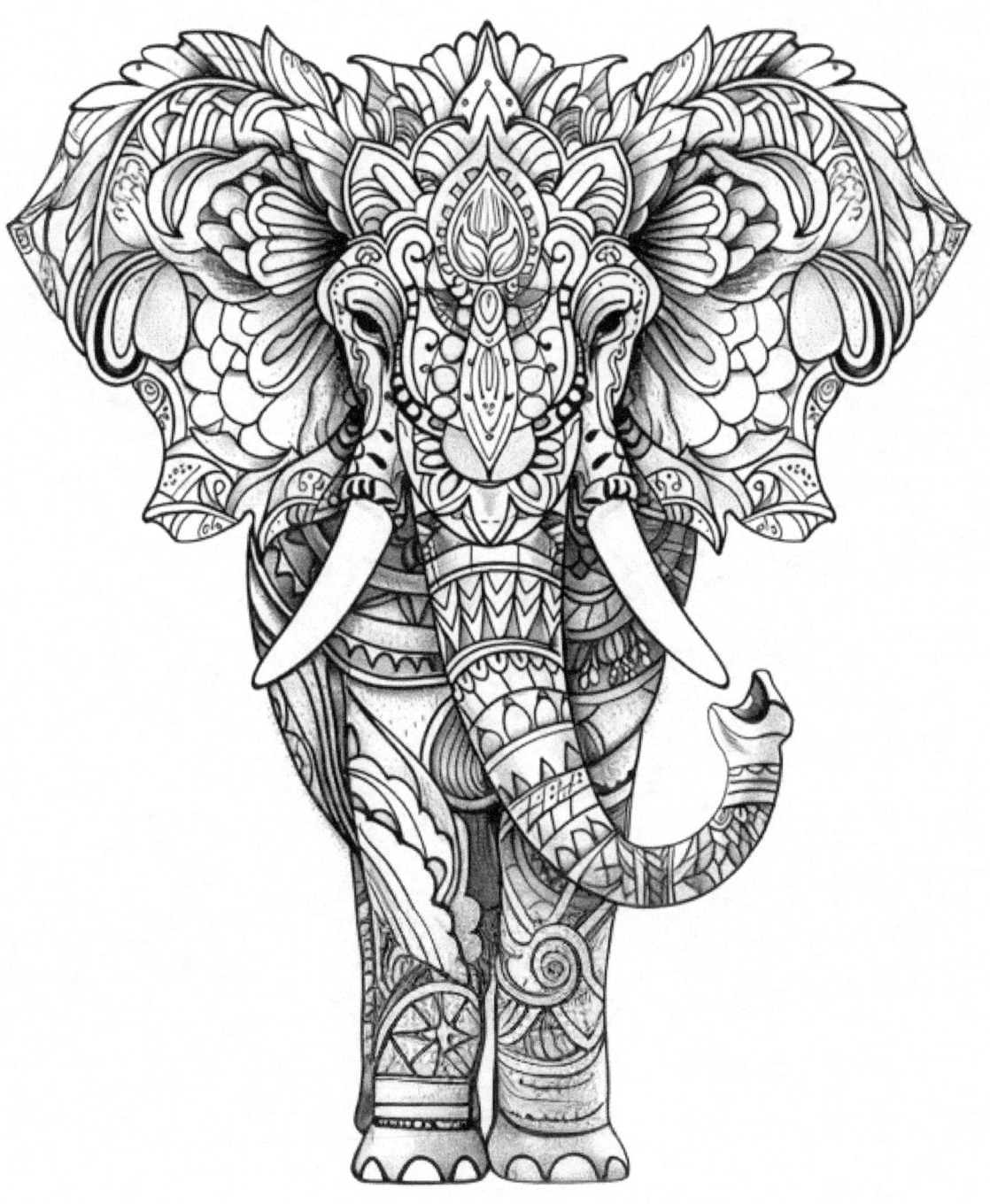

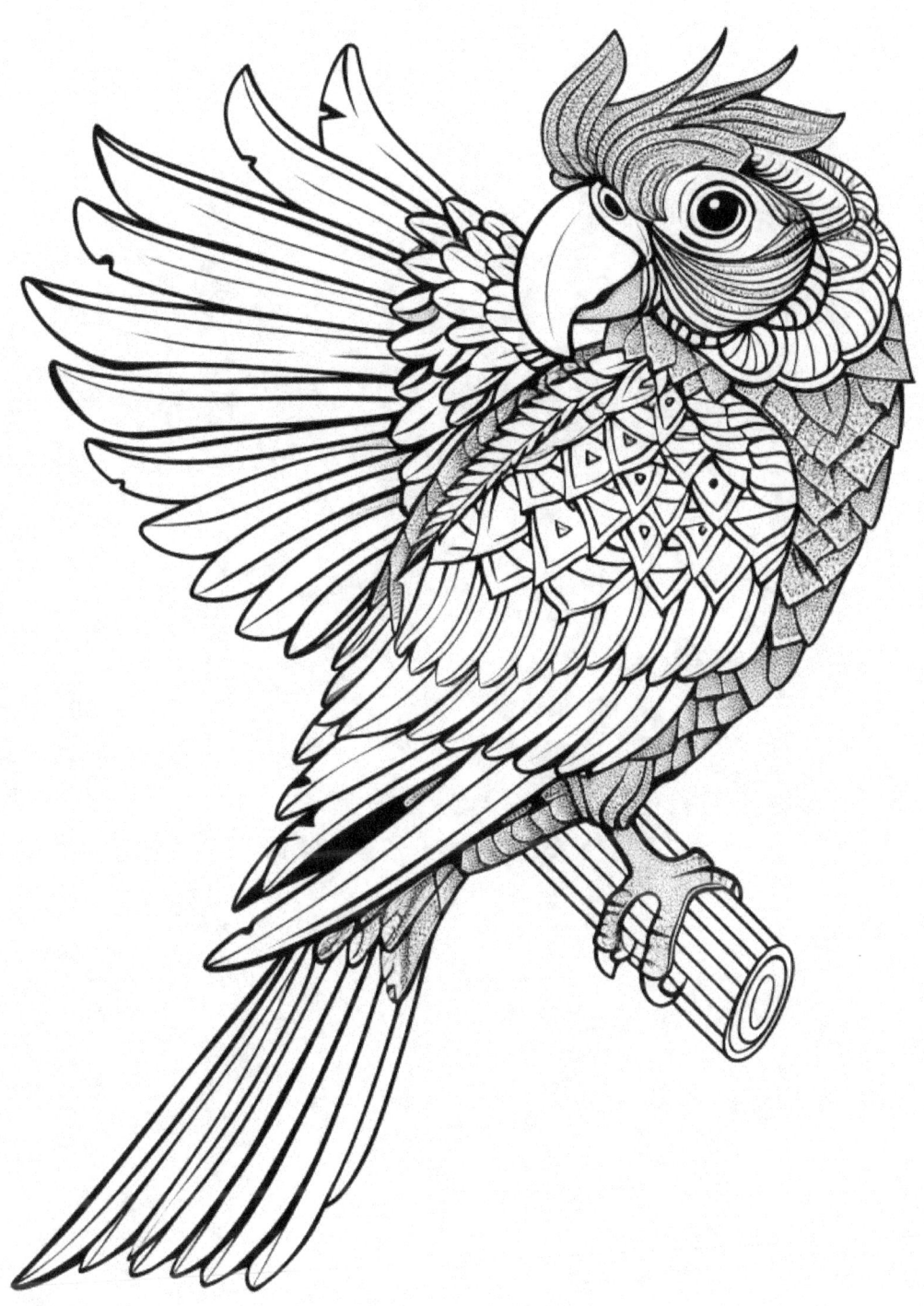

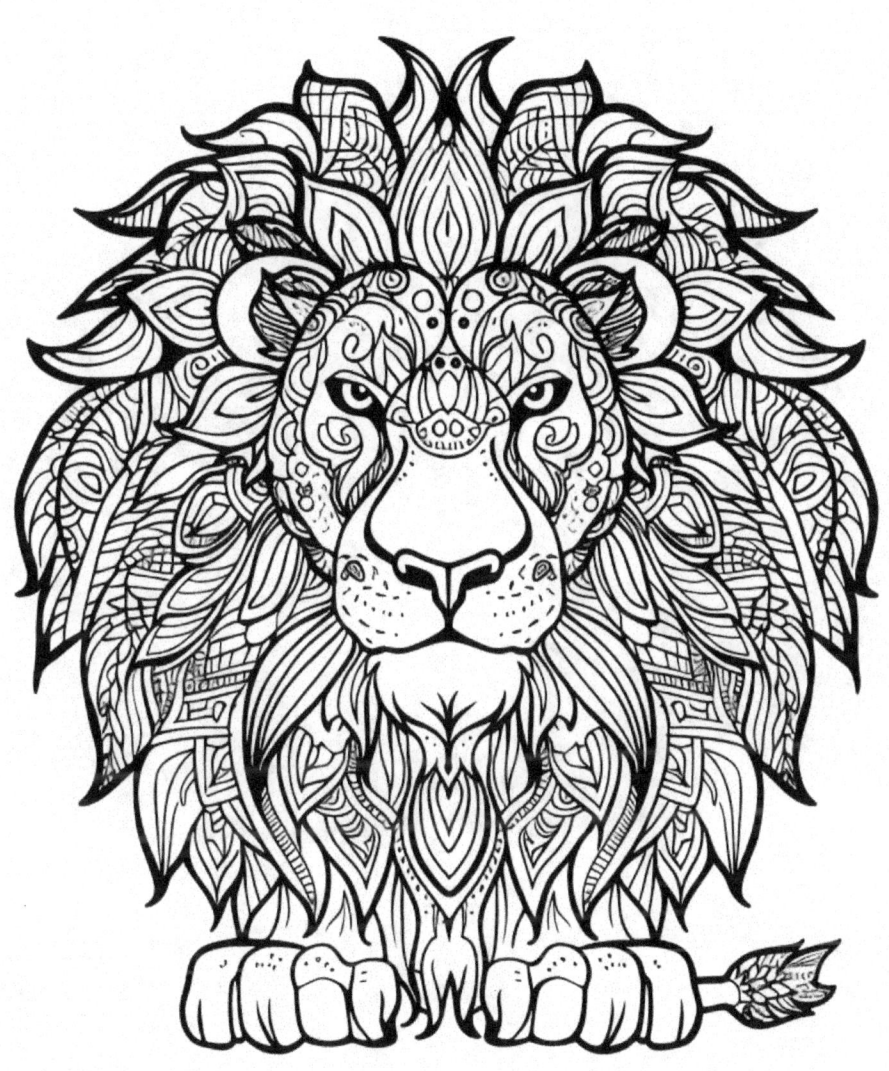

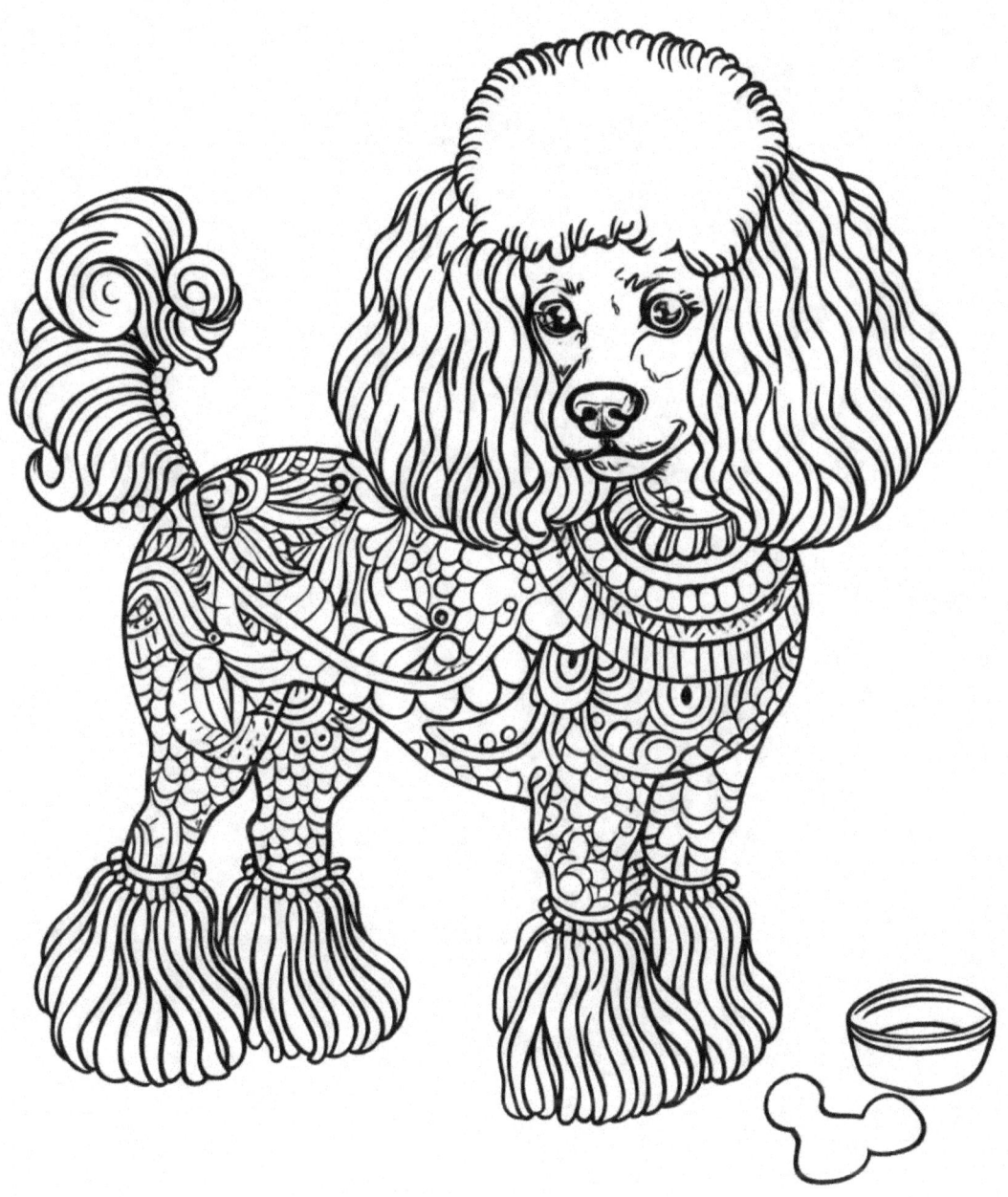

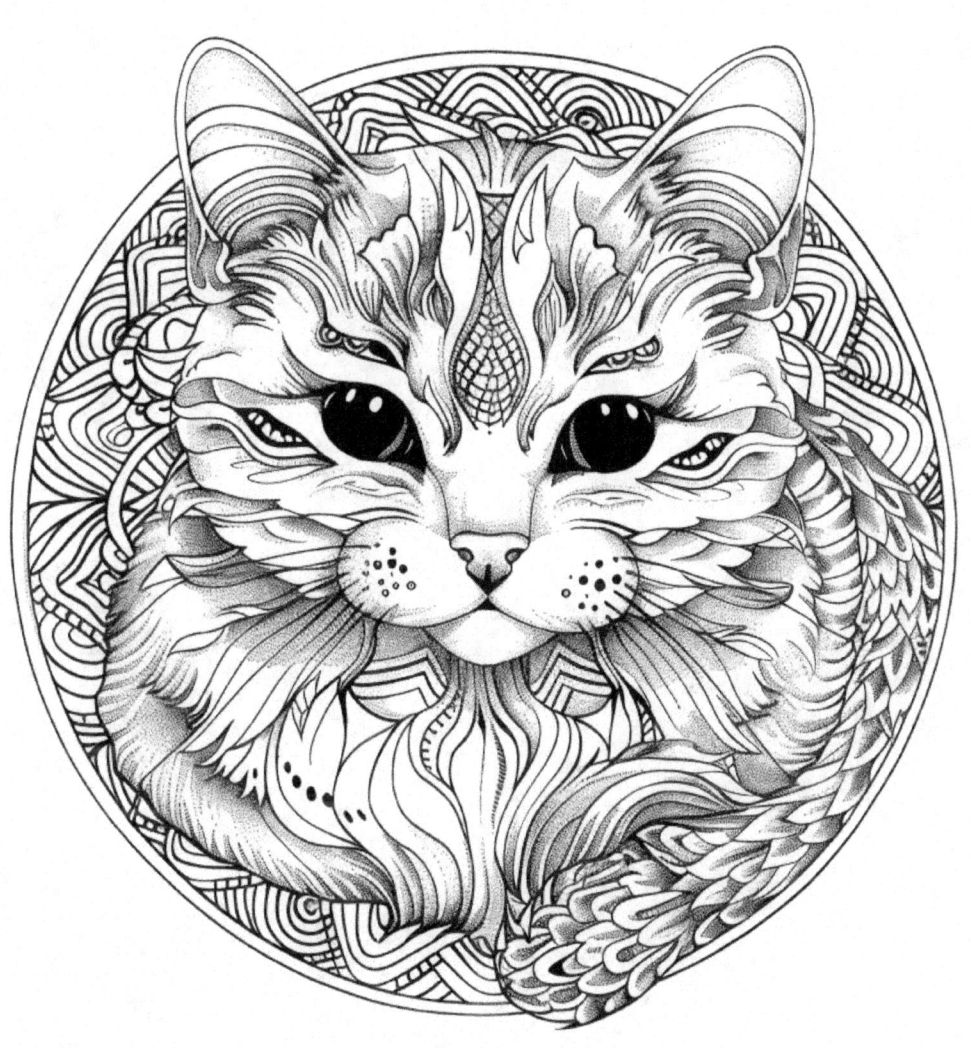

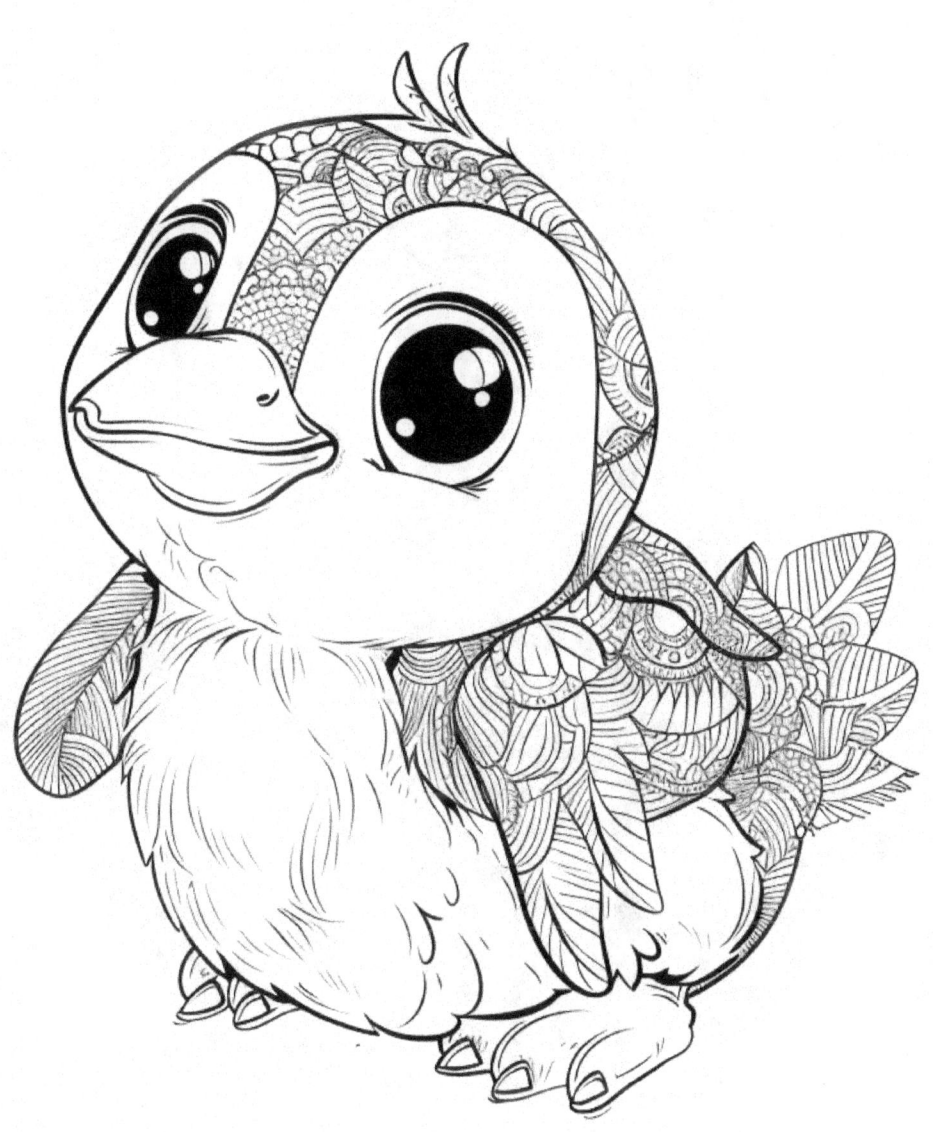

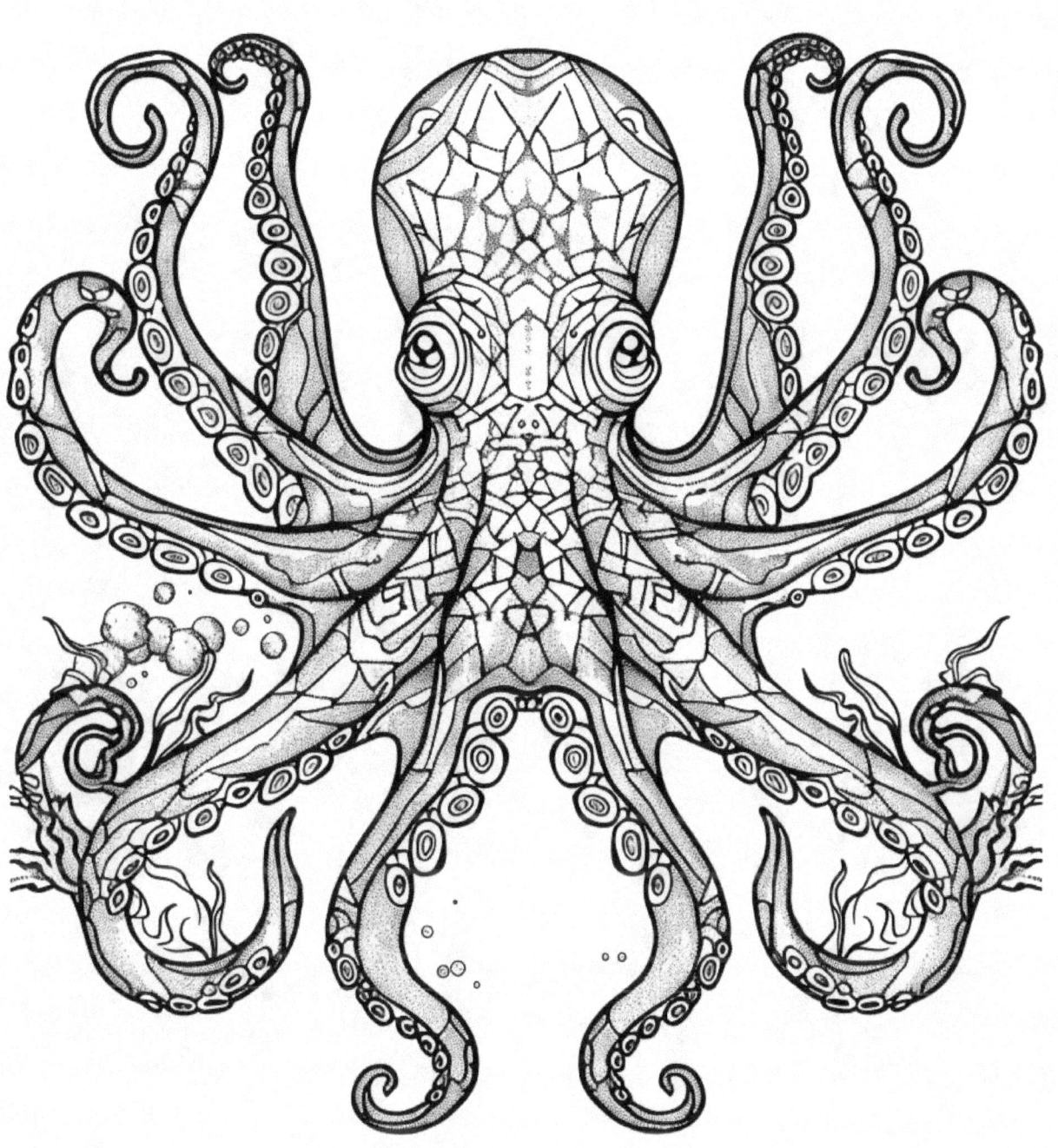

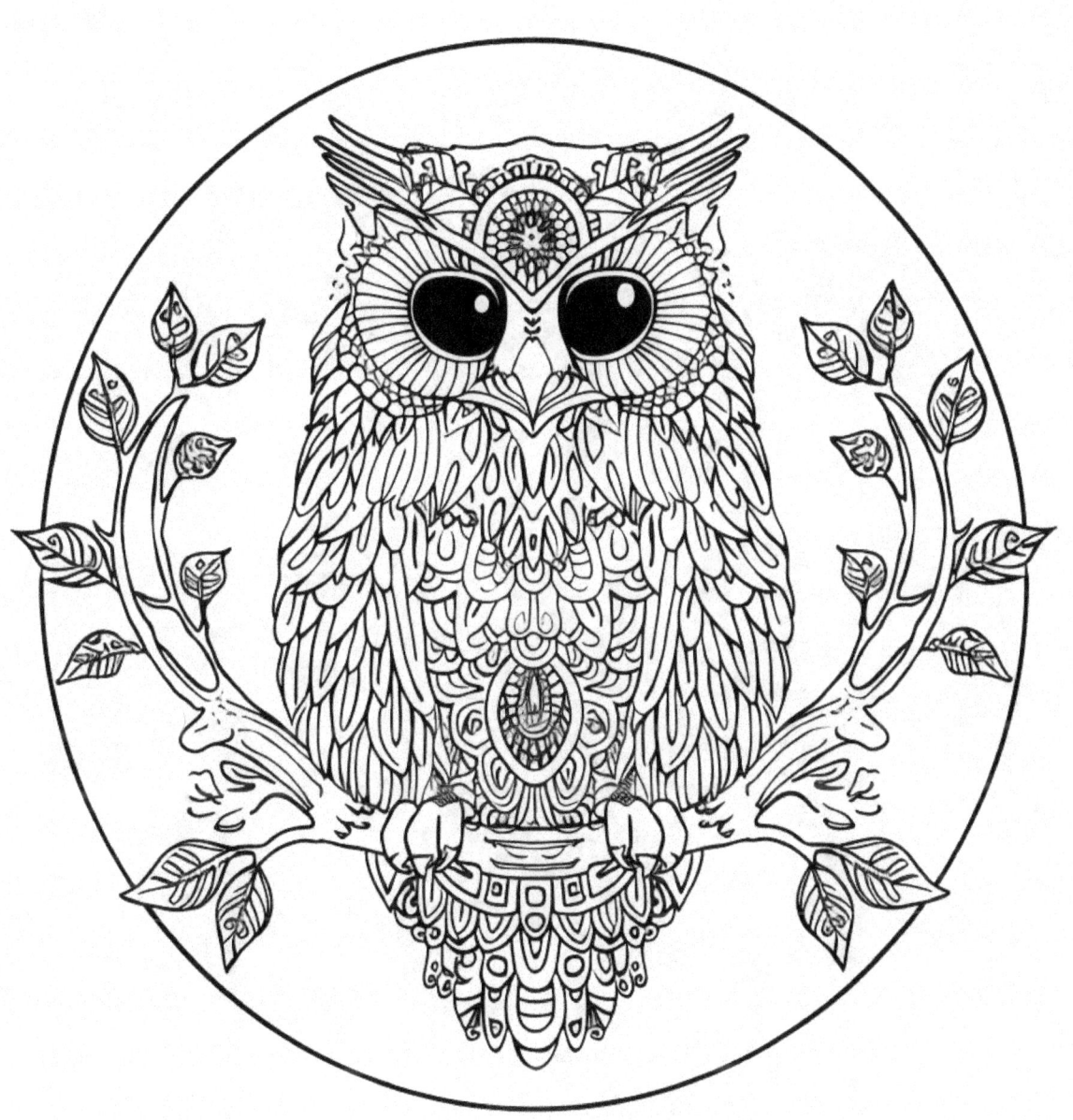

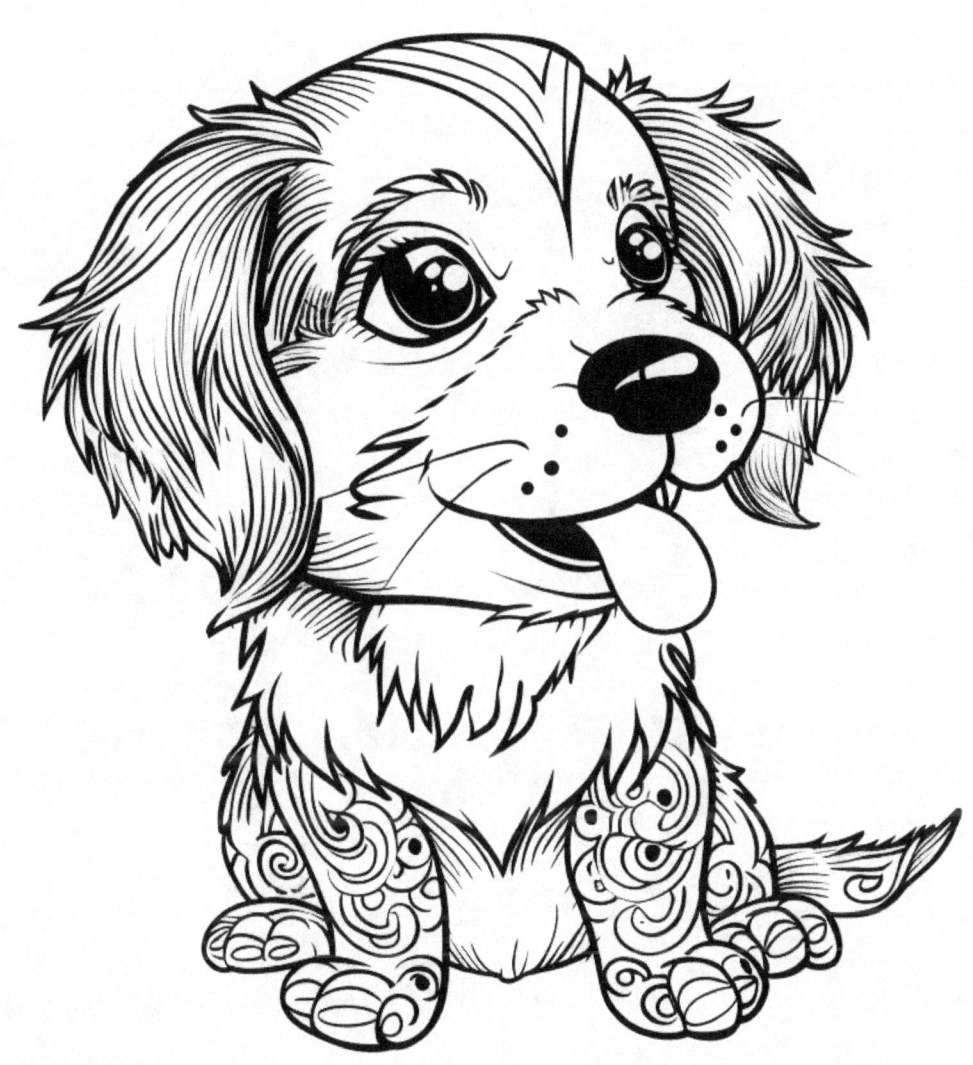

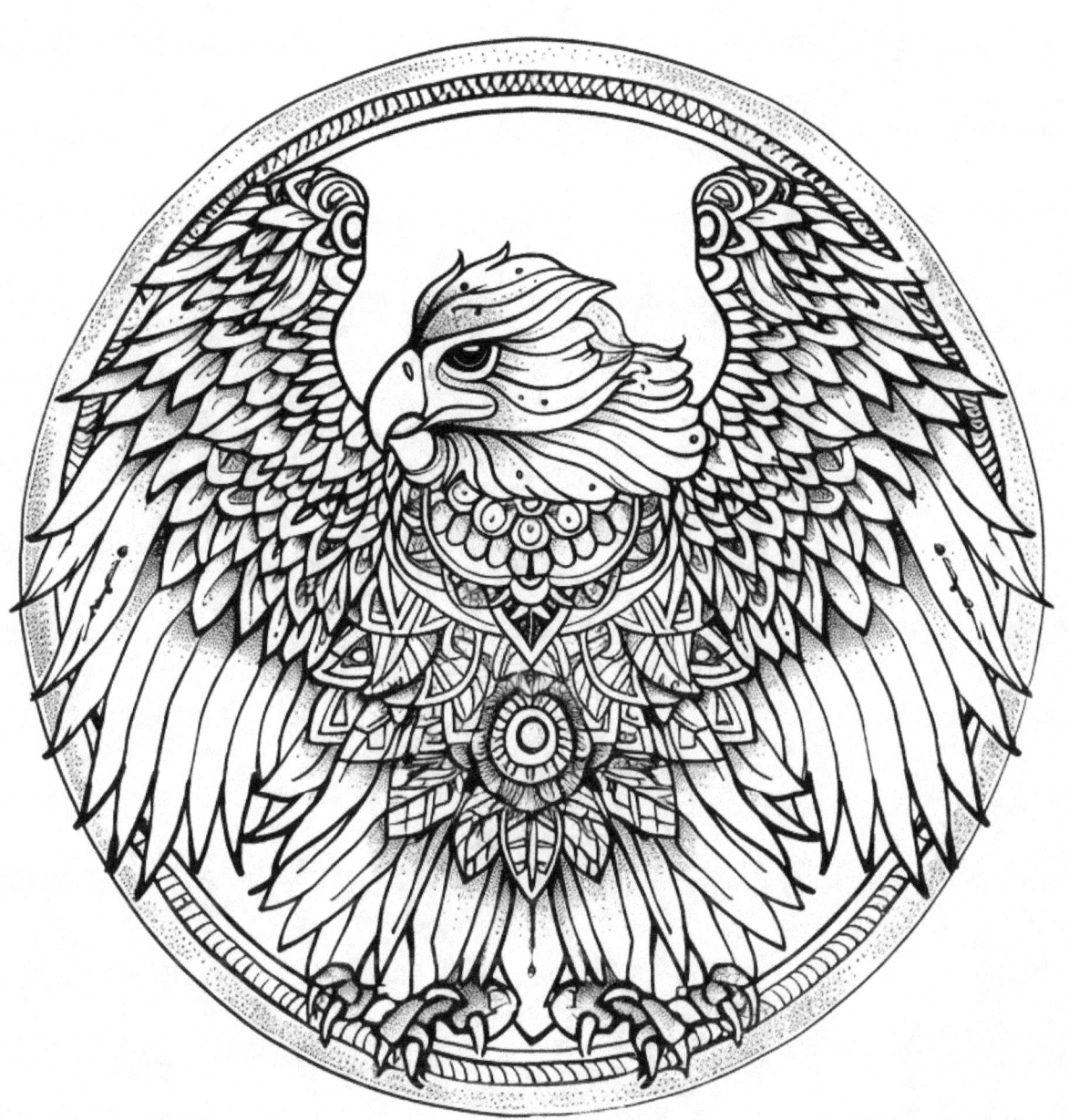

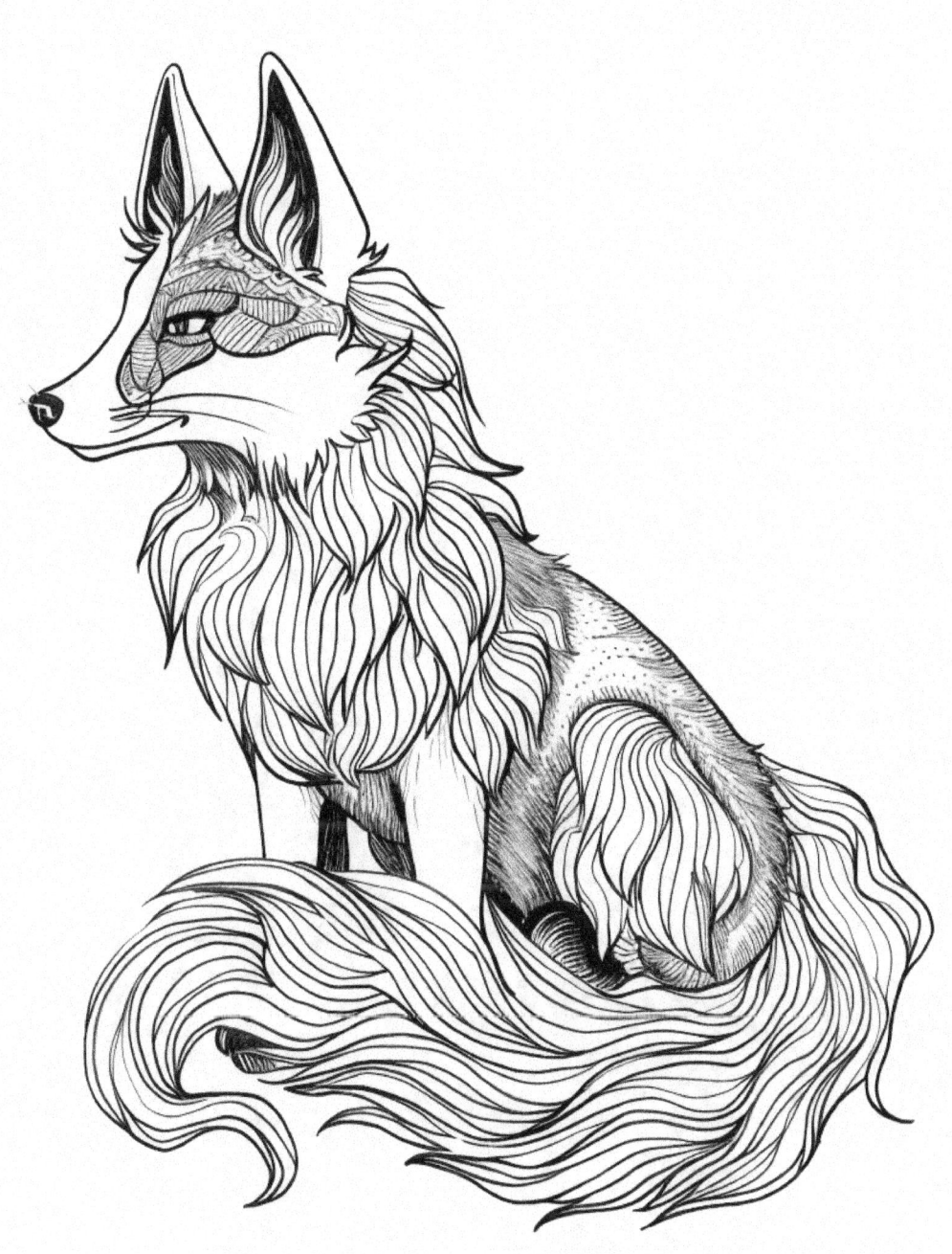

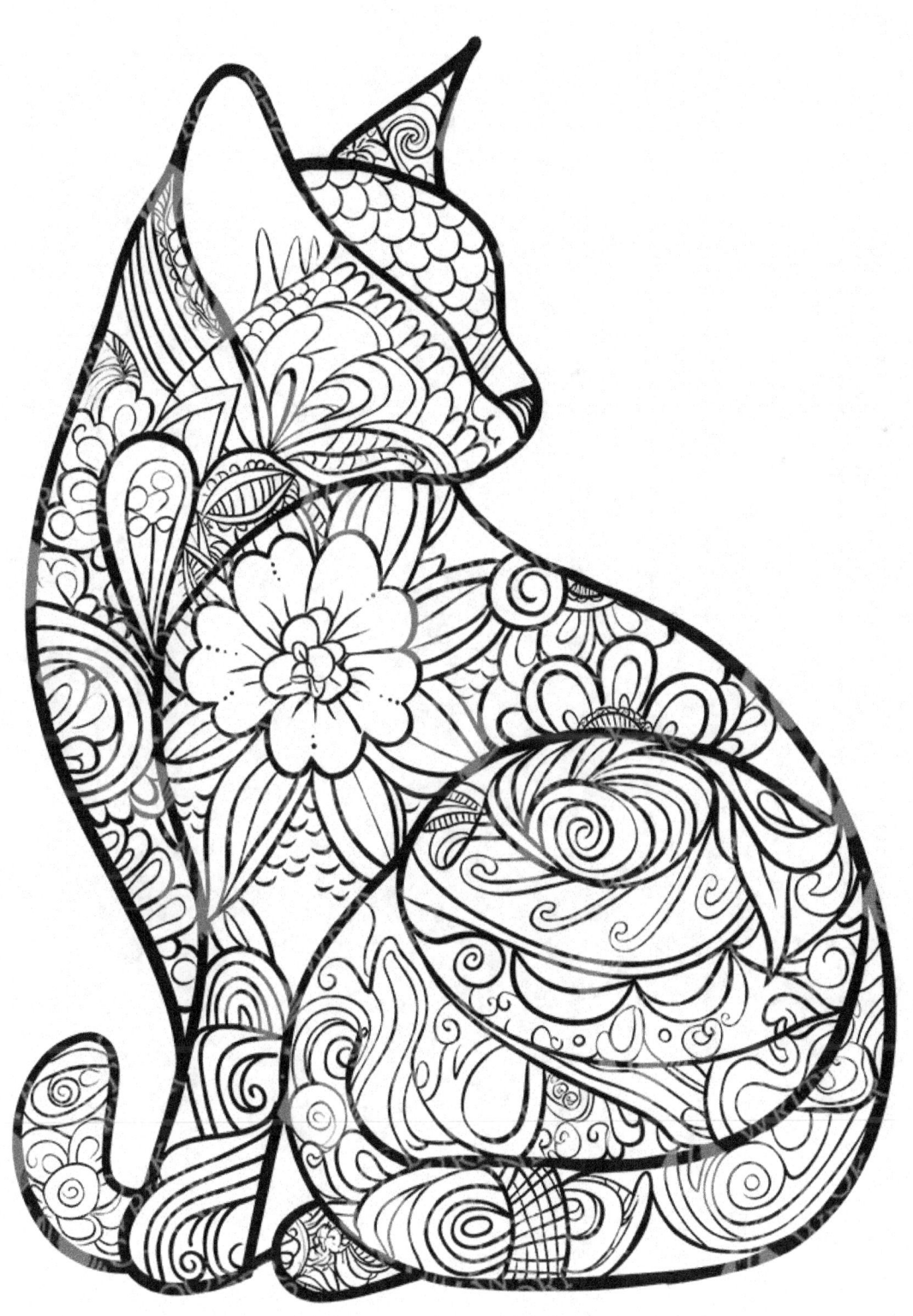

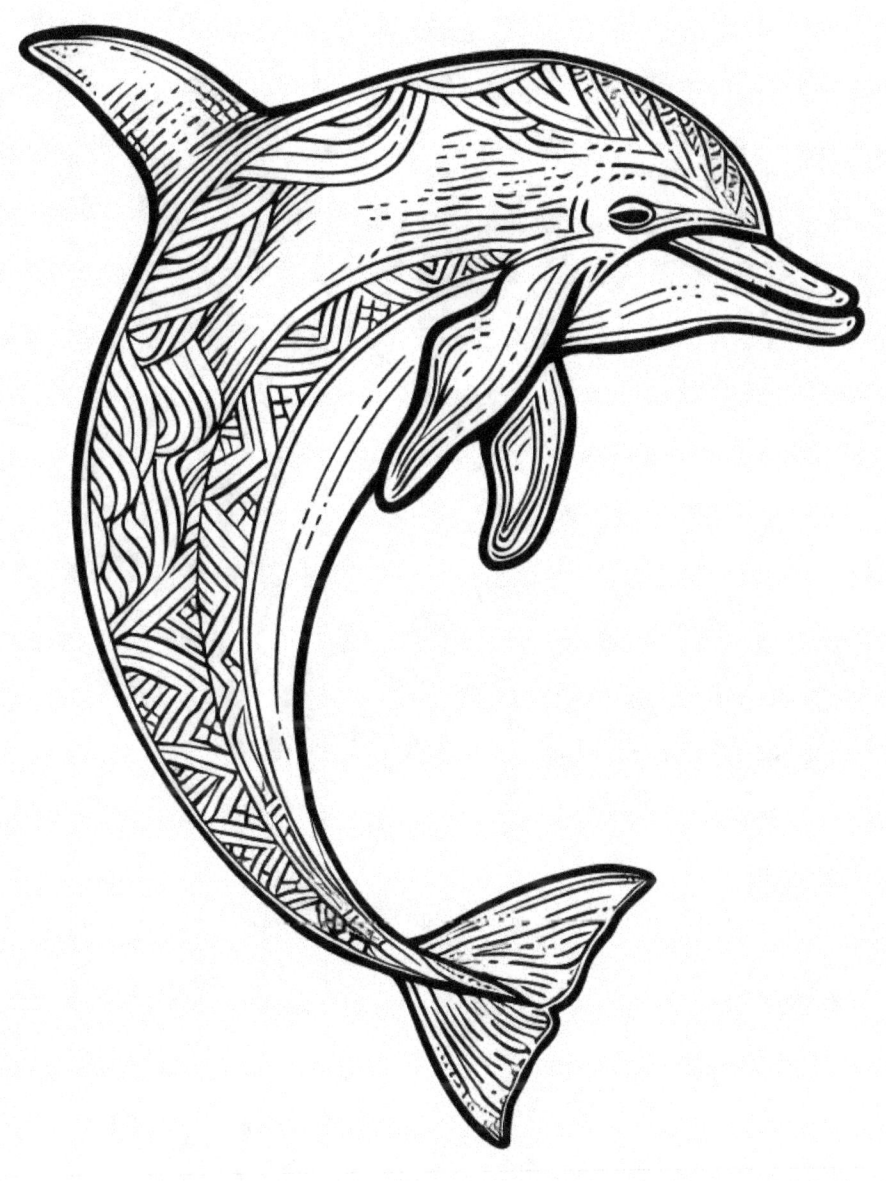

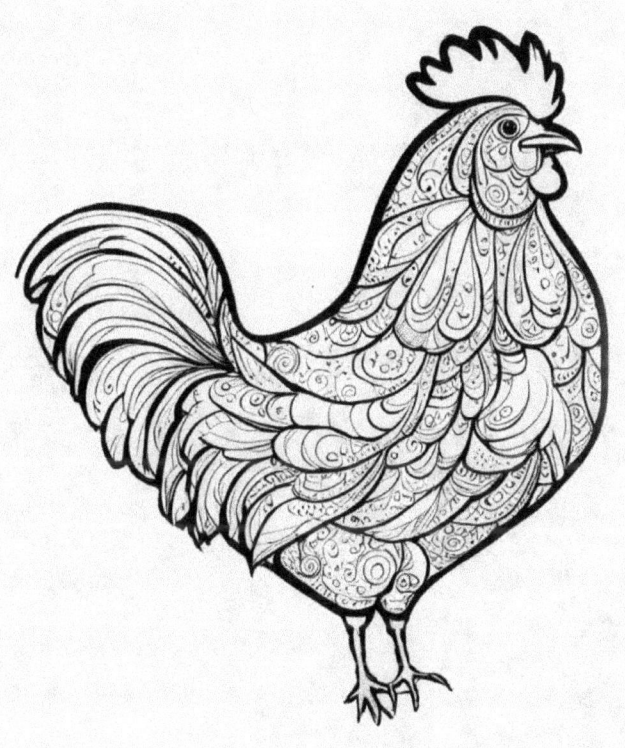

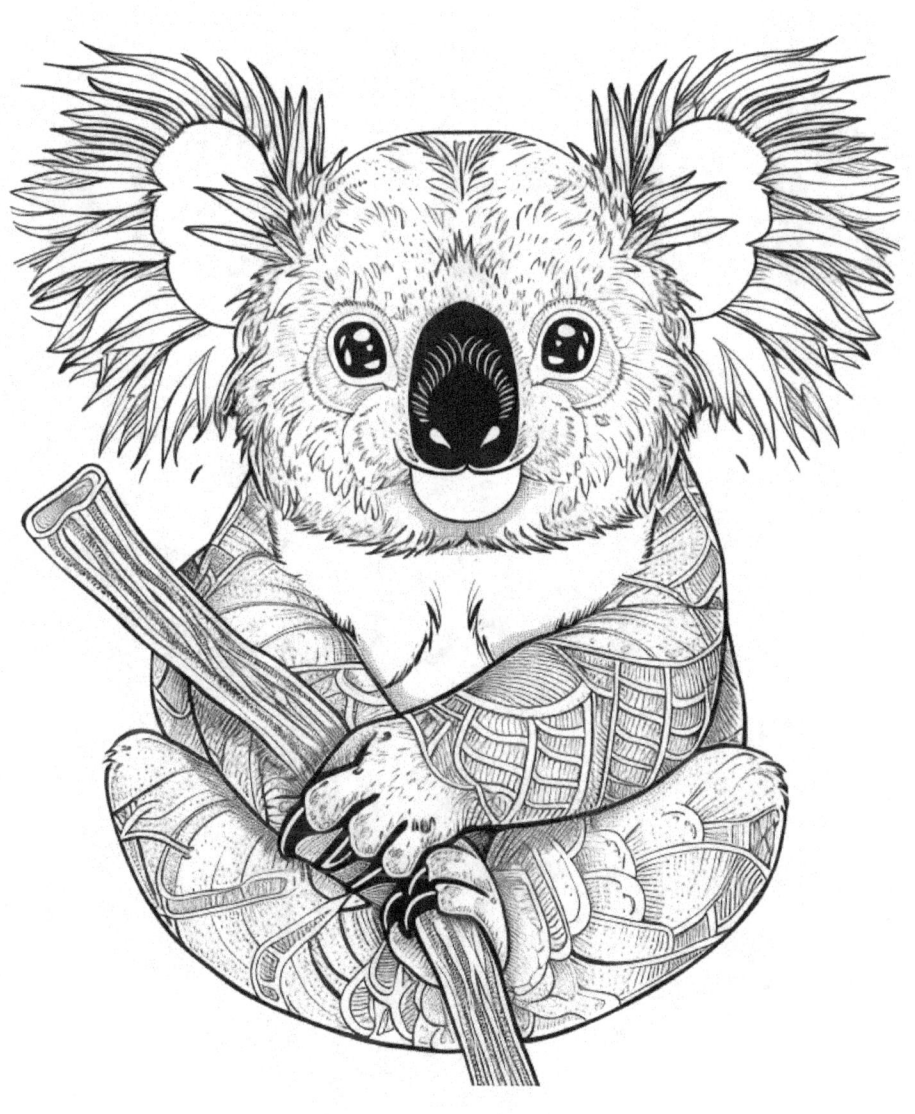

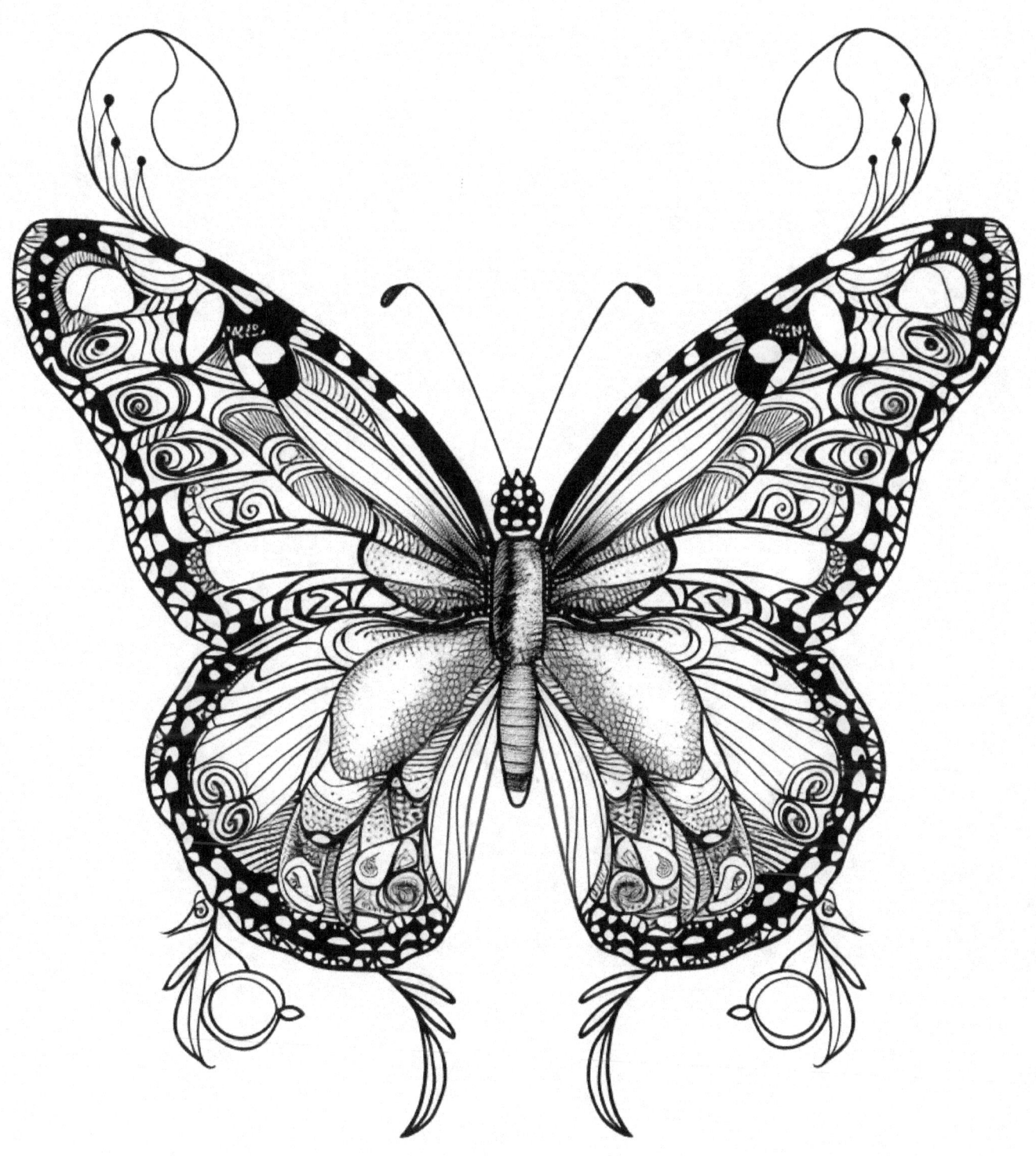

www.ingramcontent.com/pod-product-compliance
Lightning Source LLC
Chambersburg PA
CBHW081643220526
45468CB00009B/2537